To Stefan and Roland, with love from Caroline

Author Caroline Pitcher
Illustrator Jenny Arthur
Editor Clare Weaver
Designer Alix Wood
Consultant Anne Faundez

Publisher Steve Evans
Creative Director Zeta Davies

Sandy Creek
122 Fifth Avenue
New York, NY 10011

ISBN 978 1 4351 1657 3

Library of Congress Control Number: 2008011792

Printed and bound in China

10 9 8 7 6 5 4 3 2 1

Home, Sweet Home

Caroline Pitcher

Jenny Arthur

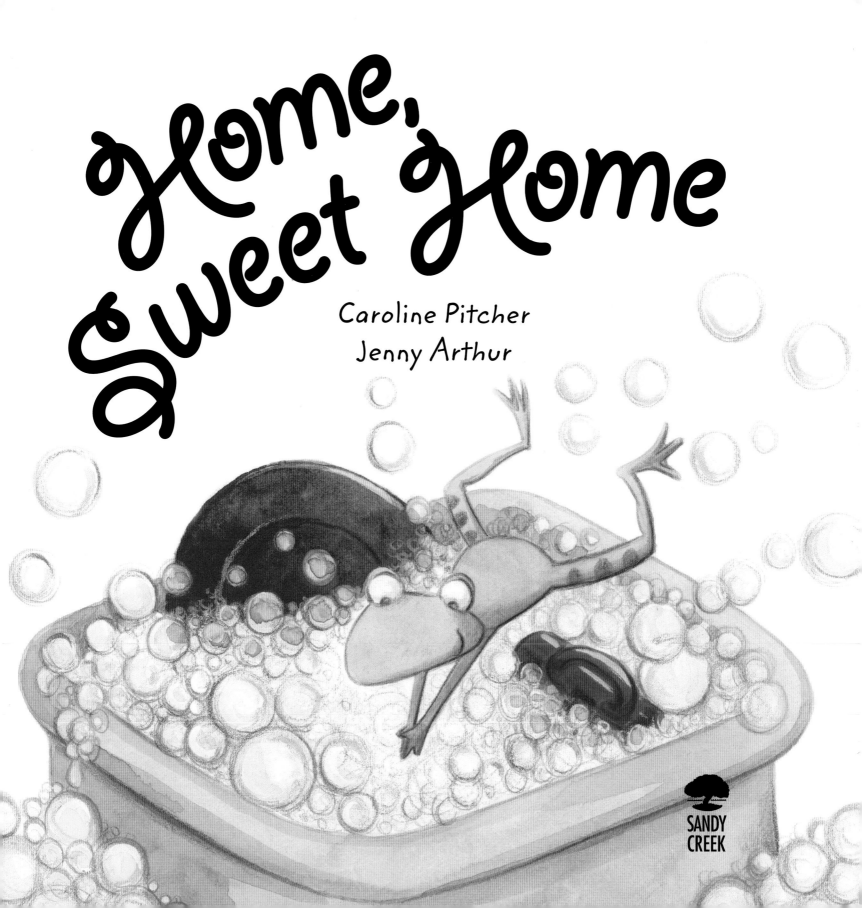

SANDY CREEK

Under the hedge was a big, green bucket with holes in the sides and water in the bottom.

In the bucket lived a frog.

One sunny day, Frog was keeping nice and cool and damp in his shady bucket.

Then suddenly the bucket **moved!**
Frog saw a large hand holding the
handle, and a **big voice** boomed:

This old thing
will have to go!

"Then so will I!"
croaked Frog, and
off he hopped to
find a new home.

It was a bad day to look for a new home.
The sun was shining and Frog felt hot.

He leaped into the rainwater barrel, but it was empty.

Ow!

He hopped toward a flowerpot,
but someone already lived there.

"No frogs allowed in
here!" squeaked Mouse.
"You're too damp."

Frog hopped under a pile
of leaves, but someone
already lived there, too.

"No croakers in my house,"
grumbled Turtle.
"You'll keep me awake."

Frog saw a cool, damp hole under a tree, and looked in.

A little face with bright eyes, a pink nose, and long whiskers popped up.

"No room in here," said Rabbit, wiggling her nose. "There are ten of us already!"

Frog hopped over to a drainpipe.
Someone with eight long legs
climbed down to look at him.

"You can't come in here,"
said Spider.
"You'll make a mess of my
perfect web!"

Frog hopped away gloomily.
Nobody seemed to want him.

"Perhaps I'll find a home here," he said, as he jumped up a step,

hopped through a doorway,
and into a kitchen.

PLOP! He dived into the dish tub, but he did not like the bubbles.

SPLASH! He hopped into the water jug, but he did not like the ice cubes.

Frog gazed into the washing machine. His eyes popped as he watched the water **whizz** around and around.

"I don't want to be THAT clean!" said Frog.

Frog hopped upstairs and into the bathroom.
"Oooh! Lots of places here," he croaked.

He leaped into the sink,

but there was no water in it.

Then Frog heard running water.

He looked around and saw water pouring into an enormous bathtub.

In he hopped.

Ouch!

"Too hot for me!" he croaked.

Frog hopped downstairs and out of the house.
The sun was even hotter. Poor Frog's skin felt dry.

He scrambled down the hot
path toward the shed.

He'd never been so far before.

"Oh, for a cool new
home!" he cried.

He hopped into the shed for some shade.
And there in a corner was a beautiful
bucket with some water in the bottom.

"It's just like my old one.
Home, sweet home!"
croaked Frog, as he
jumped in with relief.
The water felt nice and
cool on his skin.

Frog was so tired from all his hopping and searching that he fell fast asleep.

But he soon woke up when the bucket began to shake!

"Oh no, not again! I don't want to go anywhere," he croaked. "I've only just moved in!"

Frog slurped from side to side as the bucket
swung through the air. Then it stopped.
He scrambled up to the edge and peeped over.

"What very **big** boots!"
he croaked.

Frog and the water hurtled out of the bucket.

"It must be a dream... I am a flying frog!"
he croaked as he flew through the air...

down, down, down...

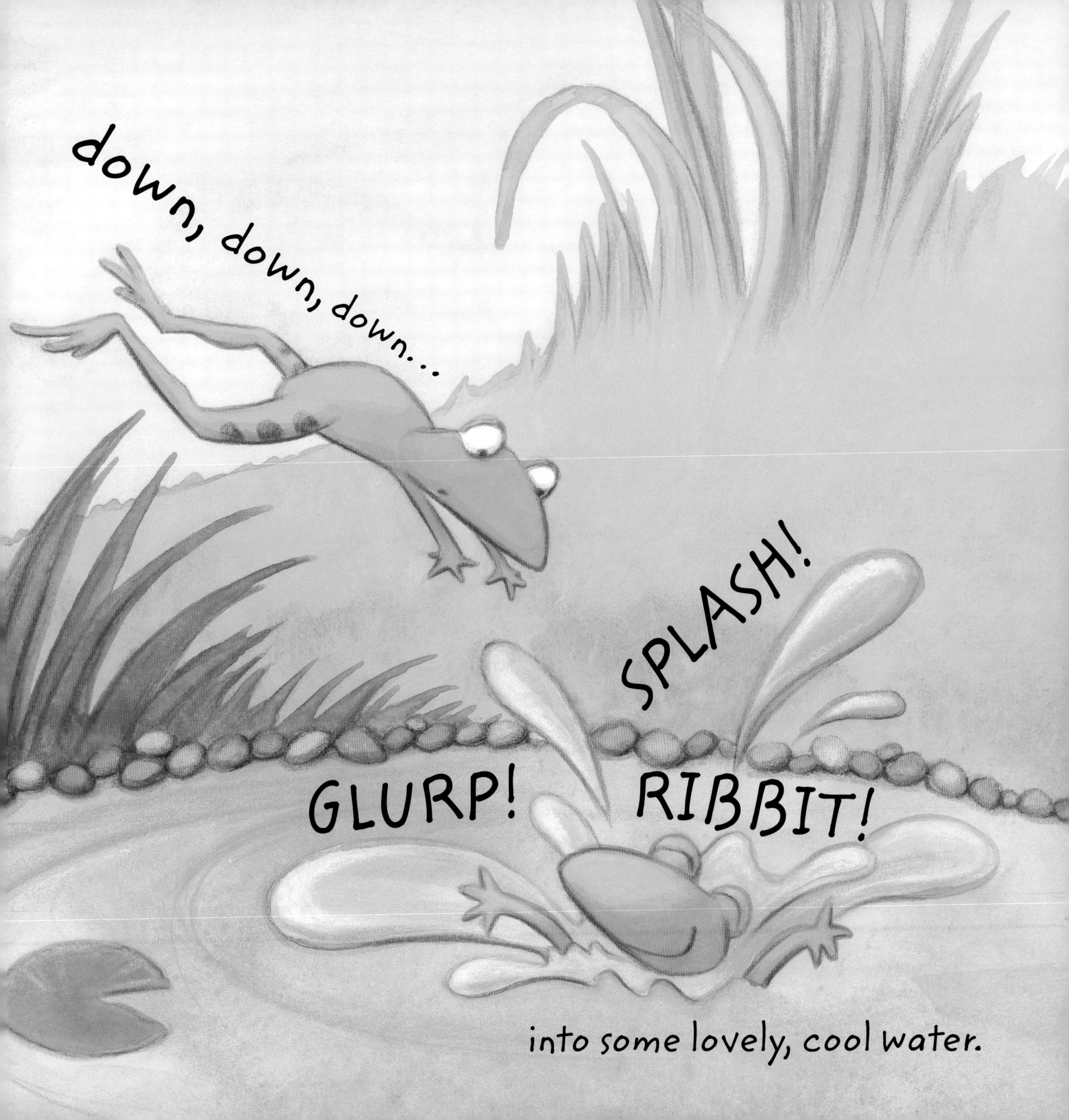

into some lovely, cool water.

Frog swam to a large lily pad, pulled himself up and sat there, gazing around in wonder.

"I can't believe my luck," he said.
"This is the most beautiful home I have ever seen!"